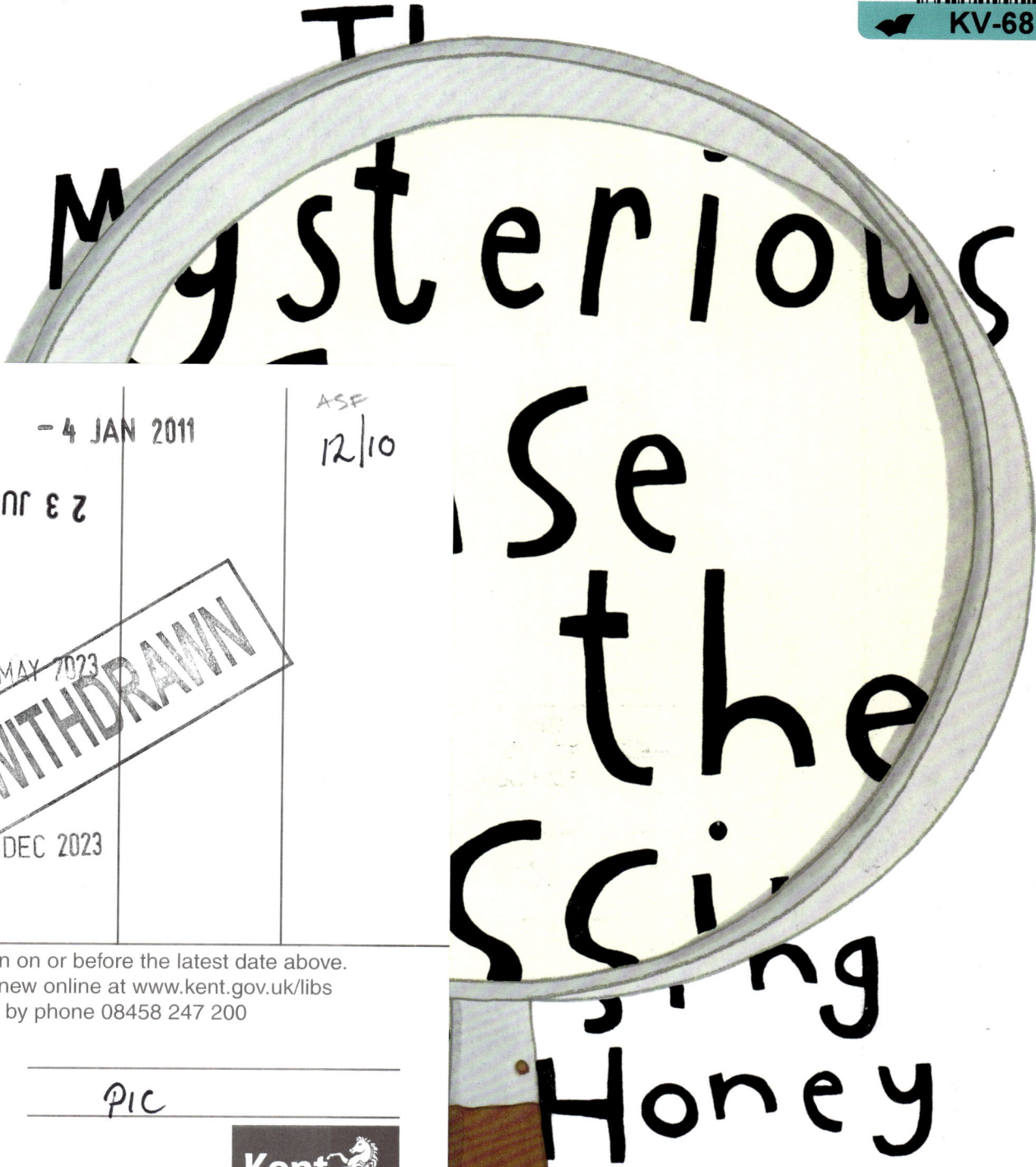

# The Mysterious Case of the Missing Honey

CLAIRE FREEDMAN

illustrated by

HOLLY SWAIN

To Liz, Jonathen and Gabriel, BFF!
C.F.

For Alice and Matilda, with love x
For Jerry-babes, my Clueless inspiration –
though not at all clueless!
H.S.

First published in Great Britain in 2010 by
**Gullane Children's Books**
185 Fleet Street, London, EC4A 2HS
www.gullanebooks.com

1   3   5   7   9   10   8   6   4   2

Text © Claire Freedman 2010
Illustrations © Holly Swain 2010

ISBN: 978-1-86233-744-2 (hb)
ISBN: 978-1-86233-786-2 (pb)

Printed and bound
in China

# The Mysterious Case of the Missing Honey

Claire Freedman

illustrated by
Holly Swain

GULLANE
CHILDREN'S BOOKS

It was a busy Monday at the police station.
Telephones were ringing! Computers were computing!

# Tring! Tring!

Inspector Clueless picked up his phone
for the tenth time that morning.

WANTED!

WANTED

boujxi

"Mr Bear here," said the voice down the line. "Help, someone's stolen my honey!"

Inspector Clueless called to his dog, Sniff-It-Out. "Sniff! There's been a theft at Mr Bear's house. Let's visit the scene of the crime!"

Mr Bear was waiting by his garden shed.
"I keep my honey in here," he pointed.
"I bought ten new honey pots yesterday.
But when I looked this morning
I found two had been
**eaten overnight!**"

Inspector Clueless inspected the shed.
Sniff-It-Out sniffed it out. Two honey pots *were* empty.
"Hmm," said Sniff. "This must be the work of a clever honey thief."
"Don't worry," Clueless nodded. "We'll get to the bottom of this horrible crime!"

Inspector Clueless and his dog rushed back to the police station.

"Fetch all our files, Sniff,"
Clueless cried. "Let's get to work!"
They looked through every file
of every suspect they knew.

Possible Suspects

SUSPECTS STRIPED
SUSPECTS SPOTTED
SUSPECTS WHITE
SUSPECTS GREEN

SUSPECTS MARINE
SUSPECTS BURROWING
SUSPECTS LONG FUR
SUSPECTS WOOL
SUSPECTS SCALES
SUSPECTS FEATHERS
SUSPECTS FUR-SHORT

NABBIT
THE RABBIT

TRICKY DICKY
CHAMELEON

BILLY THE KID

BEAK THE
SNEAK

FINGERS
THE FROG

SLIPPERY
SAM
LIZARD

STRETCH
GIRAFFE

CLARENCE
THE CAT
BURGLAR

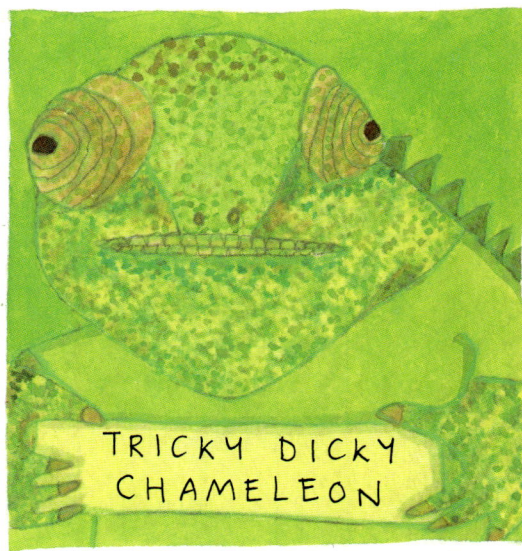

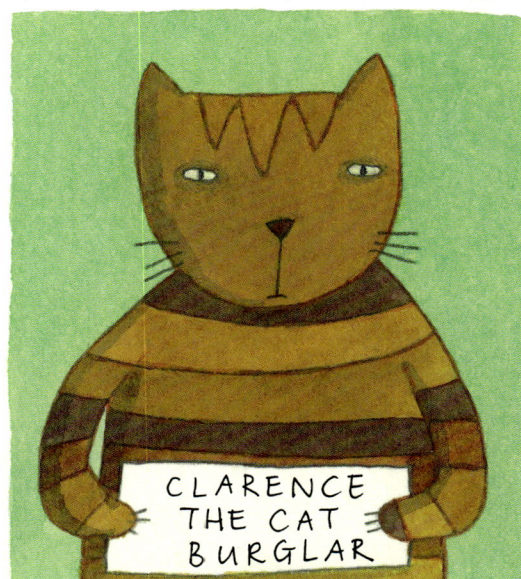

Two names stood out.

**NABBIT THE RABBIT** and **FINGERS THE FROG**.

"Let's see what Nabbit the Rabbit is up to, first!" said Clueless.

It was a dark night.
Inspector Clueless and his
dog were hiding outside
Nabbit's home.
"Nothing's happening,"
grumbled Sniff.
"Ssh!" hushed the Inspector.

Suddenly Nabbit slunk out
of his house, wearing a strange disguise.
"I bet Nabbit's on his way to Mr Bear's house, to steal more
honey!" whispered Sniff excitedly. "Let's follow him and see!"

As Nabbit hurried down the street, Clueless and Sniff crept close behind...

But Nabbit was hopping along to . . .

a Cabbage Patch
PARTY!

"It's a fancy dress party," gasped Sniff.
"That's why Nabbit was wearing a costume!"
"Nabbit won't be nabbing any honey tonight,"
sighed Clueless. "Let's go home."

It was a busy Tuesday at the police station.
Telephones were ringing! Computers were computing!

**Tring! Tring!**

Inspector Clueless picked up his phone
for the tenth time that morning.

"Mr Bear here," said the voice
down the line. "Someone's
been at my honey again!"

"We're on our way," cried Clueless.

Mr Bear's garden shed looked just as before.
But Sniff spotted some sticky honey prints on the door.
"These prints are interesting, Mr Bear," said Inspector Clueless.
"You say two more honey pots were emptied overnight?"
Mr Bear nodded sadly. "I've only six full pots left,"
he sighed. "Who could be eating them?"
"It's baffling!" said Clueless. "But we'll find out!"

It was a dark, dark night.
Inspector Clueless and Sniff
were following their second
suspect, Fingers the Frog.

"Fingers must be our honey thief," Clueless whispered.

"Yes!" laughed Sniff. "Why else would he be out this late? We'll catch him in the act!"

But Fingers was heading for . . .

The Fantastic All-Night

# FROG HOPPING COMPETITION!

"Fingers is a champion hopper," Clueless
sighed. "If any honey goes missing tonight,
we can cross *him* off our list too."

It was a busy Wednesday at the police station.
Telephones were ringing! Computers were computing!

Tring! Tring!

Inspector Clueless picked up
his phone for the tenth time
that morning.

"Guess what?" wailed the
voice down the line.

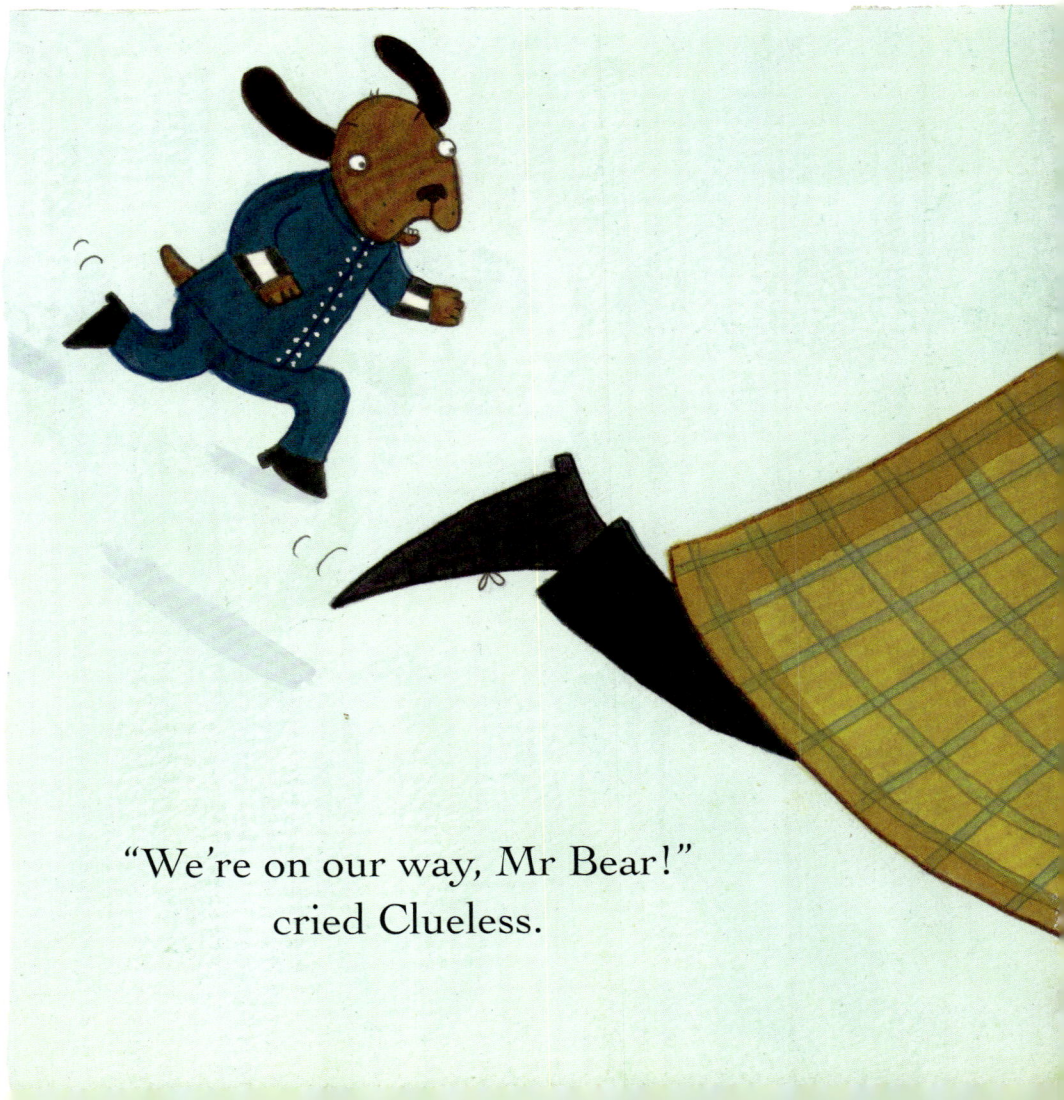

"We're on our way, Mr Bear!"
cried Clueless.

It was the same old story.
"I hurried to the shed the moment I woke up,"
Mr Bear sobbed. "Look, just one full pot left."
"Mysterious!" sighed Inspector Clueless.

"These honey prints
lead back to the house,"
sniffed Sniff. "*Whose* are they?"
"No idea," said Clueless. "This
*is* a difficult case. And we've
run out of suspects."

"Don't worry," smiled Sniff.
"I have an idea."

It was a dark, dark, dark night! Inspector Clueless and Sniff were hiding behind the shed in Mr Bear's garden. They waited . . .

and waited.

Suddenly they heard
loud footsteps . . .

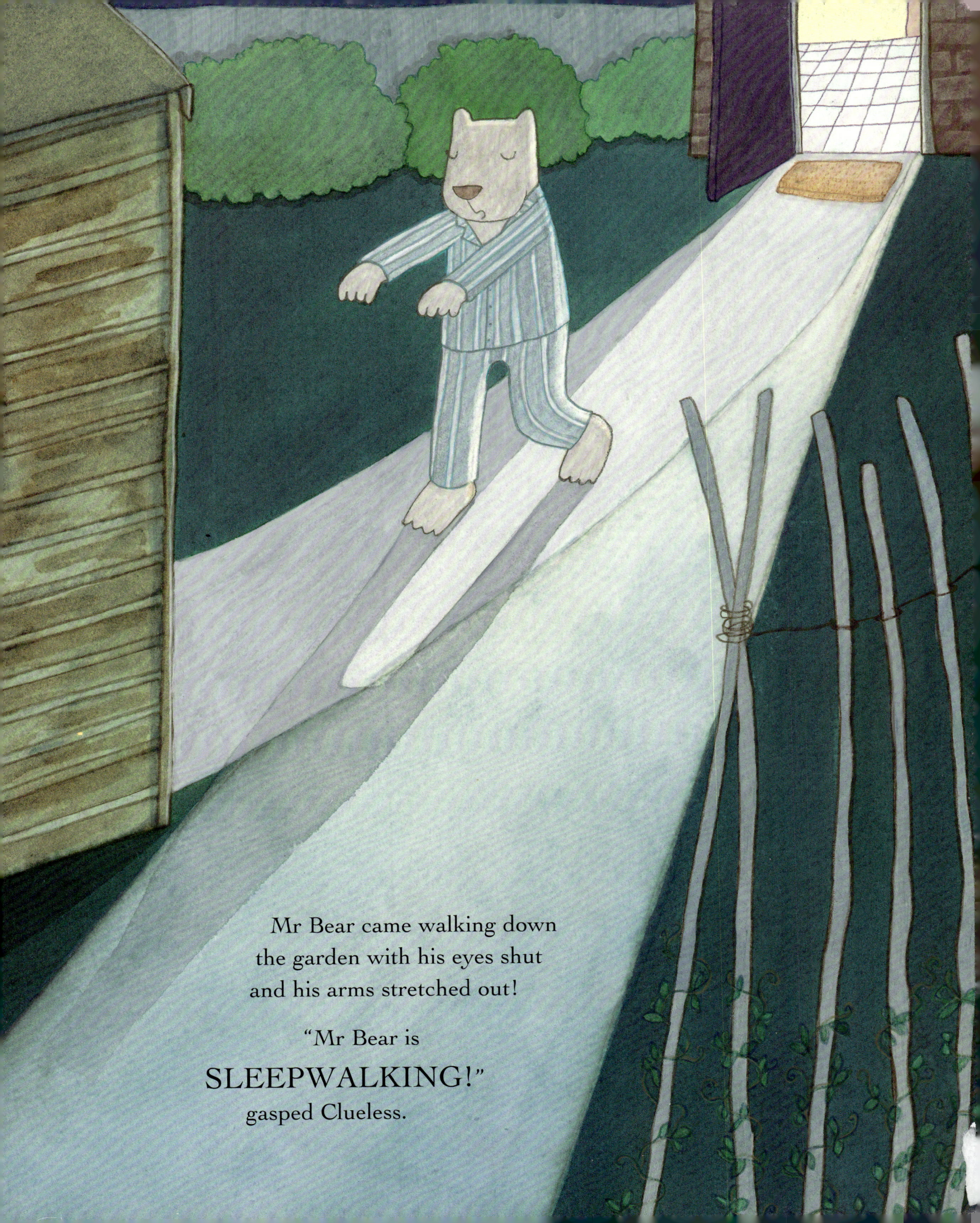

Mr Bear came walking down
the garden with his eyes shut
and his arms stretched out!

"Mr Bear is
SLEEPWALKING!"
gasped Clueless.

Mr Bear opened the shed door
and reached for the honey, when . . .

WHOOOOOAH!

He slipped.

"HELP!" cried Mr Bear, suddenly waking up. "WHERE AM I?"
Luckily, Inspector Clueless and Sniff explained everything.

"You've been stealing your own honey
**in your sleep,**" Clueless said.
"Those sticky paw prints were
yours all the time," Sniff added.
"Oh!" Mr Bear nodded. "That explains
the honey in my bed! Well done
for solving the case!"

Clueless beamed.
"Eat a snack before bedtime, Mr Bear,"
he said. "That should help. Goodnight!"

It was a busy Thursday at the police station.
Telephones were ringing! Computers were computing!

# Tring! Tring!

Inspector Clueless picked up his phone for the tenth time that morning.

"Hello, Mr Squirrel," he shouted. "Missing nuts, eh?" Clueless slammed down his phone. "Sniff," he called excitedly. " Drop everything! We've got another case . . ."